GW00498617

Clarinet
Grade 7

Pieces
for Trinity College London exams

2017-2020

Published by
Trinity College London Press Ltd
trinitycollege.com

Registered in England
Company no. 09726123

Copyright © 2016 Trinity College London Press Ltd
Second impression, June 2018

Printed in England by Caligraving Ltd

La fille aux cheveux de lin

arr. Emma Johnson

Claude Debussy
(1862–1918)

murmuré et en retenant peu à peu

Prelude no. 1

from *Dance Preludes*

Witold Lutosławski
(1913-1994)

Prelude

from *Suite from the Victorian Kitchen Garden*

Paul Reade
(1943-1997)

Tarantella

Max Reger
(1873-1916)

Caoine*

2nd movement from Sonata op. 129

Charles Villiers Stanford
(1852-1924)

* An Irish Lament, pronounced 'Keen'.

20

In Rhythm

no. 3 from *Pocket Size Sonata* (no. 1)

ed. Emma Johnson

Alec Templeton
(1910-1963)